The frog and the paddling pool

Written and illustrated by
Philippa Davies

Grosvenor House
Publishing Limited

One sunny morning, Rosie woke up and looked out of the window.

Her Daddy was already in the garden mowing the lawn.

"Shall we get the paddling pool out today?" he called up...

"It's going to be a very hot day!"

While Rosie got changed, her Daddy
fetched the paddling pool from the shed.
Then, she went outside and watched as
he blew and *blew* and *BLEW* until
the paddling pool was full of air.

Next, he fixed a long yellow hose to the
garden tap and gave Rosie the other end,
telling her to hold tight.

A moment later, Rosie's Daddy turned on the tap…

Suddenly water started shooting out of the hose!

When the paddling pool was full, Rosie's Daddy turned off the water. "Well done!" he said. Rosie smiled. "Please can I get in now?!" She was very excited.

Rosie ran across the garden and did a HUGE jump into the middle of the pool...

SPLASH!

Rosie kicked her legs and pretended to be a fish. After that, she pretended to be a mermaid.

It was sunny all day, so Rosie was allowed to play in the paddling pool right up until tea time.

She wore a special hat to protect her head from the sun, and the water helped to keep her cool.

Rosie had the best day in the paddling pool.

Then it was time to go indoors.

While she was having tea, Rosie asked if she could play in her paddling pool again the next day.

Rosie's Daddy had already checked the weather forecast and saw that it was going to be sunny all week. So he told her she could and that he would leave the paddling pool out in the garden overnight, ready for the morning.

Rosie was very pleased.

When it was time for bed, Rosie's Daddy read her a magical story about giants and mountains and rainbows...

And soon, she fell fast asleep.

The next day it was sunny again.

After breakfast, Rosie got ready as fast as she could. She went out into the garden and looked over at the paddling pool.

Rosie was just about to run across the grass and do another big jump, when suddenly – she stopped. She could see something moving. It seemed to be jumping up and down.

Rosie crept closer…

It was dark green, with big bulging eyes.

Rosie crept closer still…

It puffed out its cheeks like balloons.

Then it said something...

The frog scrabbled and slipped against the side of the pool. It jumped up and down again.

Rosie realised the frog was stuck. It must have jumped into the paddling pool during the night, but the sides were too slippery for it to climb out.

Poor frog.

Rosie bent down and gently tried to lift the frog out of the water. But it was frightened. It kept swimming away from her.

Rosie tried to think what she could do to help. Perhaps she could make a little ramp for the frog to climb up...

But what could she use as a ramp?

"Aha!" said Rosie. She remembered there was a pile of old tiles next to the shed.

Rosie carefully fetched a tile and put it into the paddling pool, with one end resting on the side. She stepped back and crouched down to watch…

After a few minutes, the frog swam across the pool and tried to climb up the ramp.

But the tile was too slippery and he kept sliding back into the water.

"Hmmm," said Rosie.

This time, she went and asked her Mummy for an old cereal box from the recycling bin, then swapped it with the tile.

But the water soaked into the cardboard and the box went all soggy. Oh dear!

Then, Rosie had another idea. She went to see her Daddy in the garden shed.

"Daddy, please can I borrow a piece of wood?"

The shed was full of interesting old things like tin buckets and plant pots and garden tools.

Rosie's Daddy passed her a wooden plank from the back of the shed. She carried it over to the paddling pool, where the frog was still splashing about.

Rosie took out the soggy cereal box and carefully balanced the plank against the side of the pool.

She stepped back and crouched down again to watch…

After another few minutes, the frog swam across the water to the bottom of the wooden ramp.

Slowly and carefully, the frog climbed up the plank.

When he got to the top, he stopped and looked round at Rosie.

"Ribbit!"

Rosie smiled. The frog smiled back.

Then, he jumped down to safety and hopped off into the bushes...

Later that day, Rosie's friends George and Lola came over to play. They brought their swimming things, so they could all go in the paddling pool together.

While they were splashing around, Rosie told them all about the poor little frog and how she had bravely rescued him from the pool.

"I know," said George,
"Let's play a game.
It's a special jumping game."

"And it's called..."

"Leap Frog!" cried George, as he hopped right over Lola's head and landed on the grass next to the paddling pool!

"Yay!" said Lola...

"Hooray!" said Rosie...

"Ribbit!" said a voice from somewhere in the bushes...

Lightning Source UK Ltd.
Milton Keynes UK
UKHW050434110822
407149UK00011B/112

9 781803 810652